**VESTAVIA HILLS
PUBLIC LIBRARY**

1112 Montgomery Highway
Vestavia Hills, Alabama 35216

Our one-hundredth book
for none other than
our parents
—*Elle and Erik*

For Anna
—*MvH*

Text copyright © 2008 by Elle van Lieshout and Erik van Os
Illustrations copyright © 2008 by Mies van Hout
Originally published under the title
Schatje en Scheetje by Lemniscaat b.v. Rotterdam, 2008
All rights reserved
Printed in Belgium
First U.S. edition, 2009

ISBN-13: 978-1-59078-660-4

CIP data is available.

Lemniscaat
An Imprint of Boyds Mills Press, Inc.
815 Church Street
Honesdale, Pennsylvania 18431

Lovey and Dovey

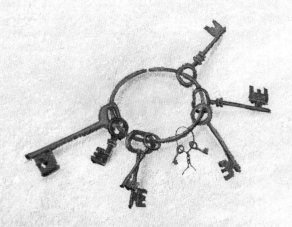

Lovey

Elle van Lieshout & Erik van Os
Mies van Hout

and Dovey

Lemniscaat
Honesdale, Pennsylvania

In the deepest, darkest, most dismal dungeon
of Katakom, there were once two robbers,
Lovey and Dovey. They had stolen
each other's hearts.

    And a pair of blue socks
from the sock shop on the corner.
That's why they were now in prison.

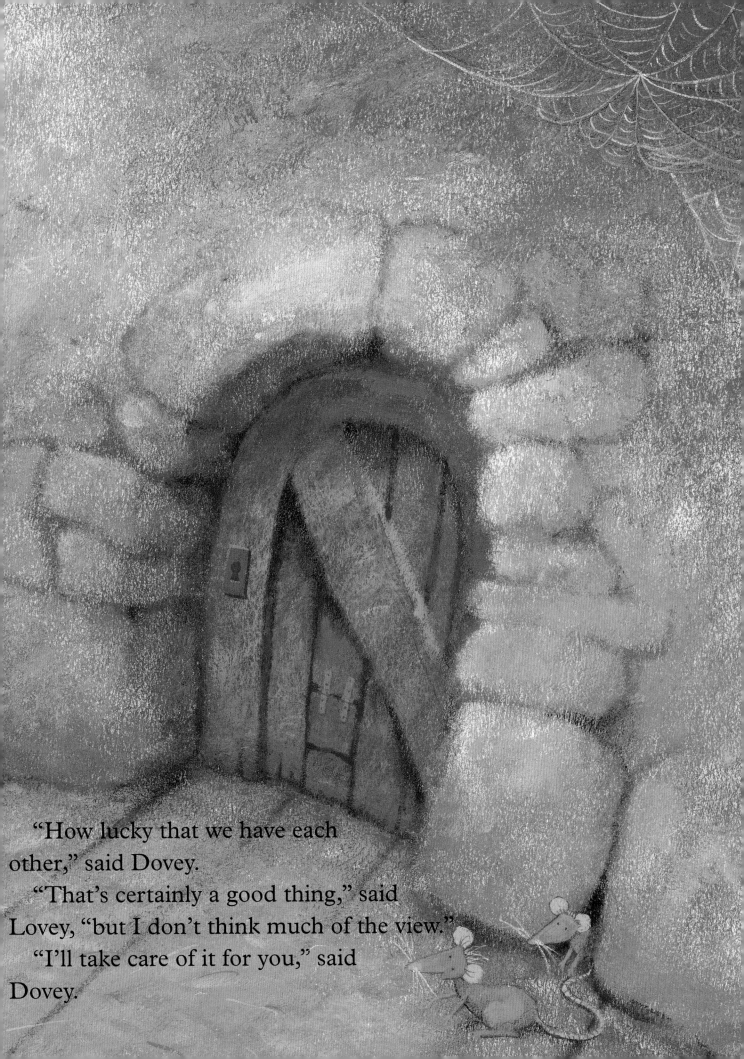

"How lucky that we have each
other," said Dovey.

"That's certainly a good thing," said
Lovey, "but I don't think much of the view."

"I'll take care of it for you," said
Dovey.

He sized up the big, gray wall
and squeezed his way through the bars.

Dovey went looking for sun and sea ...

... and came back with a
beautiful view over his shoulder.
He hung the view on the wall.
It looked just right.

That same evening, they lay on their
thin blanket. They were staring at the ceiling.
No stars, no moon, just concrete.
    Dovey made a lasso with his rope and set off.
"I won't be long, Lovey."

He flung his lasso into the air
and caught a crescent moon
and a whole star-spangled sky.

Back in the dungeon, Dovey released his catch.
The moon and the stars rose. Under the sky that
had been stolen with love, they fell peacefully asleep.

The next morning, their breakfast was pushed through a hatch in the door.

"Boring!" said Lovey. "It's bread and water again!"

"Just a minute," said Dovey. Off he went …

… and came back with some juicy treats. "For you, Lovey."

Every night, Dovey went out
stealing. And he always came back
with something lovely.

"We're pretty snug here," said Lovey.
"You can say that again!" said Dovey.

But one day, disaster struck:
they were released.

"Come on, Lovey," said Dovey, and he pulled her
along to the sock shop on the corner.
They waited until the police officer saw them.

The police officer was looking! At that very moment, they stole one pair of pink socks.